Edward Blackadder

Poems: Sonnets, Lyrics, and Miscellaneous

Edward Blackadder

Poems: Sonnets, Lyrics, and Miscellaneous

ISBN/EAN: 9783744772082

Printed in Europe, USA, Canada, Australia, Japan

Cover: Foto ©Andreas Hilbeck / pixelio.de

More available books at **www.hansebooks.com**

POEMS:

SONNETS, LYRICS,

AND

MISCELLANEOUS.

E. BLACKADDER.

HALIFAX:

NOVA SCOTIA PRINTING COMPANY.

1895.

INDEX.

PROEM.

TO MY FRIENDS.

DEAR FRIENDS, herein the fruits of many an
    hour,—
  Haply far wiser spent,—behold, I lay
  Before you as a tribute ! and would say,
Lo ! these were plucked what time the Muse's power
Brought back to me,—a not unwelcome dower,—
  The many-featured memories of the past ;
  And too, the spoil of passing moments cast
On me in many a sweet and saddening shower.

Grant, then, oh Muses, thy weak child to make
  Worthy the offering of these lispéd lines,
Wrought in bright times when joys were all awake,
  Or when the gloom of life the soul confines
Sad as the moonbeams on a silent lake,
  Deep forested in darkly shadowing pines.

PROEM.

TO MY FRIENDS.

DEAR FRIENDS, herein the fruits of many an
    hour,—
    Haply far wiser spent,—behold, I lay
    Before you as a tribute ! and would say,
Lo ! these were plucked what time the Muse's power
Brought back to me,—a not unwelcome dower,—
    The many-featured memories of the past ;
    And too, the spoil of passing moments cast
On me in many a sweet and saddening shower.

Grant, then, oh Muses, thy weak child to make
    Worthy the offering of these lispéd lines,
Wrought in bright times when joys were all awake,
    Or when the gloom of life the soul confines
Sad as the moonbeams on a silent lake,
    Deep forested in darkly shadowing pines.

Sonnets.

AUXILIUM AB ALTO.

I saw, in visioned sleep, a mortal tread
  Upon a narrow islet midway placed
  Within a grim abyss, where might be traced
The surge of sulphury flames and smoke that spread
Up-blown in volumes vast. All pale with dread
  He found his footing lessen more and more ;
  When, lo ! a sunburst from the clouds high o'er
Streamed down, and in its midst a golden thread.

He gazed, beheld and grasped, and from my view
  Ascended to those opening realms of light.
The Isle was Earthly Hope ; the Abyss that grew
  Destroying it, Despair, the unfailing blight
Of joys terrene ; the Golden Cord that drew
  To safety was Christ's Love, vouchsafed in sorrow's
    night.

A PIOUS FALLACY.

It gives small praise to God to call mankind
  A worm, or such, expressing littleness,
  Disparaging His own workmanship's impress.
It is poor praise to say the Eternal Mind
Holds empire over beings scarce designed
  Above non-entity ; for true it stands
  To laud the structure from the builder's hands
Is to applaud the builder ; for we find

The glories of created things reveal
  Their maker's greatness. Then what tongue can say
Man is so mean, and yet in conscience feel
  'Tis honoring God ? Saith not the Sacred Lay,
" Fearful and wonderful thy Maker's seal
  Is set upon thy framing, child of clay ?"

ON A CERTAIN PROVERB.

THERE is a saying which, though meant for good,
   Is so expressed to give impressions wrong :
     That " all things come to him who waiteth long."
A proverb making most delicious food
For the dulled palates of the laggard brood,
   Or for the ill-rewarded 'tis a song
     That dims despair, though only to prolong ;
But for ambition 'tis a stumbling wood.

Wait not beside Life's swift, storm-tortured river
   For waves to fall or currents to subside,
     Or magic bark to bear thee swiftly o'er !
Plunge in the torrent's rage, nor fearful shiver !
   Buffet the billows ! on the surges ride !
     Turn not nor pause and thou hast gained the shore.

FROM "THE LOOK OFF."

I STOOD upon the mountain's towering brow,
   And viewed beneath, around, a scene sublime
     Unmatched beneath the sun in any clime :
Westward for many a league, the vale below
Lay in its loveliness, and in the show
   Of town, and stream, and wood, and meadows green,
     Afar extended till the wondrous scene
Was lost in splendours of the sunset glow.

A hamlet at my feet ; and eastward wide
   Spread the wild waters o'er their shifting sand ;
Where many a white sail passing I descried,
   That silent glided to some distant strand ;
Then straight my spirit thrilled with conscious pride
   That all this beauty was my native land.

FROM PARTRIDGE ISLAND.

GRAND as the scene that on the Patmian shore
    Rose on the vision of the Sainted Seer,
    Was that : Below expanded far and near
The majesty of waters ; southward o'er
The billows, Blomidon dark looming bore
    His shroud of mist ; and where the surges sweep
    Westward, steep frowned defiance unto steep,
While Fundy's floods fierce intervening roar.

Ships, there, full sailed or anchored in the shade
    Of promontory high or verdured isle,
Told of emprize and nation-building trade
    Which bids with bloom the arid desert smile ;
And over all, the westering day star played
    With shafts of mellow radiance the while.

ANNAPOLIS ROYAL.

A stranger here within this ancient town,—
    Long time agone the rising hope of France,
    The seed of future empire,—as in trance
'Mid storied scenes I wander up and down :
Here rise the grass-grown walls which bore the frown
    Of death-disgorging cannon long ago,
    And wide the gleaming basin spreads below,
Where thunder-bearing ships no more are known.

Yea, Death hath reaped his harvest in this place,
    Along these shores have hundreds bled and died
    To save this jewel for the Gallic crown.
But Fate ordained it for another race ;
    The sturdy Saxon tills yon meadows wide ;
    Peace rules o'er all ; War's trumpet sleeps unblown.

FATHER DAMIEN, THE LEPER PRIEST OF MOLOKOI.

OFT had I read, in annals of the past,
　Of heaviest sacrifice for Jesus' cause
　Made joyfully, and by accursed laws
How many a glorious martyr breathed his last,
Rejoicing that his humble life was cast
　　An offering on Faith's Altar ;—and I said,
　　" Alas ! faith is grown dim and fervour dead !
If asked to die for Christ, men stand aghast !"

But when, unknown to me before, I heard,
　Oh sainted Damien, thy now hallowed name,
And when across the broad Pacific, word
　Was borne that thou the martyr's crown didst claim
Fronting a horrid death to serve thy Lord
　　And suffering race, I said, " undimmed is still the
　　　flame !"

ON THE DEATH OF SIR JOHN McDONALD.

THE brightest planet of our northern sky,
　In the undimmed effulgence of its ray,—
　Our country's guide through calm and tempest play,—
Is quenched in night.　Oh ! may no patriot eye
Remain, oblivious of that greatness, dry !
　　If for his monument you'd search, survey
　　Stretching a thousand western leagues away
A youthful nation in its vastness lie.

Among the foremost ever foremost, he,
　Surpassing others, knit the band which bound
Kingdom-wide provinces, from sea to sea
　Into one giant realm.　Then bid resound
His praise, posterity, and let him be
　　Father of Canada forever crowned.

2

TO PASTOR FELIX.

Thou gentle singer of soul-touching strains,
　A dreamful sweetness born of thy strong love
　Of beauty or of mountain, field or grove
Or home remembrances, the mind retains
That reads thy page ; and of thy native plains
　The breath fans round him and his feelings roam
　In yearning back to his Acadian home,
The sunlit bays, green vales and shady lanes.

Such with the wanderer ; but whom thy muse
　Charms here at home, feel in their bosoms rise
An inspiration which can but infuse
　A new affection for their native skies ;
And future times and men shall not refuse
　To know thee in Acadia's destinies.

THE FATHERS OF ACADIA COLLEGE.

Of old, when Glory knew no other clime
　Than her own Hellas, beauteous legends told
　How many a spirit of heroic mould,
Bursting the bounds of clay and human time,
Soared upward and within the heavens sublime
　Blazed forth a constellation new enrolled
　On the celestial page, and shed the gold
Of brighter beams than in their mortal prime.

E'en so in sooth of that heroic band
　May be declared, who with no selfish aim,
　But with pure love obeying the command,
" Let there be light !" reared in the sacred name
　Of Learning, that beloved and structure grand,
　Our own Acadia of hallowed fame.

SHELLEY.

A SORROW dims my spirit when I gaze
   On ocean, wakened, answering the roar
   Of rage-winged whirlwinds in their stormy war
Smiting his form through all its winding ways.
For the stern scenes within my mind upraise
   Thoughts of *His* doom who sang the Titan free,
   In strains of more than Heaven-wrought harmony.
Wild crossed the billows in their angry maze

In Spezzia's Bay, that hour, when not afar
   From shore and friends, the faithless bark went down;
And in dim caverns deep below the jar
   Of surface thunders, cold and pale was thrown
The grandest treasure that the ocean floor
Upon its full-gemmed bosom ever wore.

KEATS.

Lush-throated songster, how our spirits rise
   And languish, as thy mild, melodious muse
   Pours forth her sweetness in a tide profuse :
Ode, epic, sonnet and symphonious sighs !
But Death, that jealous tyrant, he who tries
   All beauteous things, haled thee to his dark tower
   Ere life had fairly budded to full flower,
Hushing thy high-harped, heavenly harmonies.

Alas ! those strains, which to thy hopes, were sung
   To greet the blushes of the orient flow,
Proved the swan's note, and sadly, grandly rung
   A dirge to thy life's planet sinking low
In mists, which gorgeous form its splendours, hung
   Round the down-drooping with unfading glow.

TO H. S. DAVISON.

" *Amici donum cœli sunt.*" Of old
   So wrote the Roman. 'Tis a noble thought,
   And true as noble : It has been my lot
To feel upon this earth, so grand and cold,
The glow divine true friendship doth unfold.
   Fast friends were we in childhood's golden time,
   Fast friends while youth was budding to the prime
Of manhood, and no cloud hath ever rolled

Of enmity between us. Generous heart,
   A Christian kindness and a spirit pure,
   An energy that ever gains its end,
Will strong, a mind wherein no trifling part
   Of genius hath its dwelling-place secure,
   These are the proud possession of my friend.

LINES

WRITTEN ON SEEING A VERY PRETTY LITTLE DEAF AND DUMB GIRL IN THE TRAIN.

Sweet child with fairy form and angel face,
   I see thy dark eyes flash on all around
   With keen inquiry ; then, new interest found,
Thy glance is turned upon the flying trace
Of ever varying landscapes as they race
   With swift retreat beyond the vision's bound.
   Intense thy gaze and thy delight profound,
But ah !—those sweet slips may not part to praise.

Sunshine is for thee, and the flowers bloom
   In ever gorgeous tint to please thy sight ;
   Brooks, woods and fields, moon, stars and azure sky
Can charm, but Nature's voices all are dumb :
   For thee no song-birds warble, day and night
   One deathless silence hold, tongueless the years roll
      by.

A CHARACTER.

Smile-flashing eyes within whose azure deeps
   Lie worlds of most enchanting innocence ;
   The snow-pure brow, the sanguine lips intense
Where every love his rosy mansion keeps ;
The cheek of peach whereon a cupid peeps
   From 's dimple fortress, and the dainty chin
   A lush pomogranate ; framing all within,
The halo of her golden tresses sweeps.

My love hath all of these, but they by far
   The least of her possessions constitute,
   And are no fosterers of vanity.
Heart gentle, soul as pure as sunbeams are,
   Mind for whose beauty angels might dispute,
   These, only these are prized, sweet one, by thee.

ON COMPLETING THE PERUSAL OF "THE FÆRIE QUEENE."

As one whose soul by day is rent with care,
   At night is by a golden-winged dream
   Wafted on high where rolls the limpid Stream
Of Life, and God his flaming throne doth rear
'Mid beauty's blinding brightness, and the air
   Sweet palpitates with many a 'trancing note
   From soulful harps by angel fingers smote,
And ah ! the dreamer wakes and earth is there ;

E'en so it fares with me who late have trod
   Entrancedly along the daedal ways
   Of the honied paradise of Faerie Clime :
Cares were forgot, at rest was sorrow's rod,
   All sadness lost within that rainbow maze ;
   And now,—the earth is here and human time.

SONNET.

ON FINDING, IN AN OLD WELL, A BALL WHICH I HAD LOST MANY YEARS BEFORE.

Joy of my youth, and source of many a tear
  In being lost, I have recovered thee
  That wert unseen so long that memory
Had banished thee from her protecting care.
But now thy form recalls the day, the year,—
  That summer day,—when joyous o'er the lea
  I playing ran, thou stolest my joy from me
By vanishing adown yon darksome lair.

To-day I find thee after years have fled,
  And all my sorrow for thy loss forgot ;
Too late, such joys as thine have long been dead !
  Thou bring'st sad proof how wishes come to nought;
We longing wish for joys with childhood sped,
  Which, once returned, would fit no more our lot.

ON ATTAINING MY TWENTY-THIRD YEAR.

Thou hast been more profuse, O pauseless Time,
  In years than deeds ; but still I blame thee not ;
  Rather myself I blame because my lot
Hath not been worthy of the ripening prime ;
For I've neglected thy bestirring chime
  That urged me to the toil of deeds unwrought
  Waiting innumerable my hand.   God wot
My soul is heavy with inaction's slime !

But will my sorrow teach me in the years
  Unborn, to act a grander, nobler part,
  And bring forth fruit meet for the season's bloom ?
If it be so, in spite of all my fears,
  Those hours which heedless passed, O troubled heart,
  Have still in life been worthy of their room.

ON RE-VISITING SPINNEY'S OLD MILL.

I sought to-day an old haunt of my youth,
　Where an old mill had fallen to decay,
　Leaving some vestige of its happier day :
The crumbling dam, the wheel without a tooth,
The pond with lilies laden, silvery smooth,
　The timber raft whereon we'd often play,
　Twain apple trees, huge, gnarled, with mosses gray,
And circling all, a gloomy forest growth.

To-day the place once more mine eyes beheld,
　But ruthless Change had placed his blight on all :
　The dam was there more ruined , where the pond
Once gleamed, a growth of verdant flags upswelled ;
　The raft was stranded, rotting ; stead the pall
　Of ancient woods, smiled fields of grain around.

EDUCATION AND THE HUMAN MIND.

THERE lies a land beneath a tropic sky,
　Where the sweet sunlight, pouring ever down,
　Is but a curse and withers bare and brown
The land into a desert where the eye
May wander league on league nor yet descry
　A blade of grass, or tree, or blossom grow ;
　While bare and blasted sleeps the soil below,
Its fertile bosom blistered all and dry.

But in due season, swollen by the fall
　Of rains on th' Abyssinian mountains far,
The Nile his kindly wave spreads over all,
　And grain and fairest flowers blooming are.
That land's the Human Mind untilled and rude,
And Education the Nilotic flood.

Lyrical Pieces.

HYMN TO THE SUN.

LIFE-GIVING orb, that from the gates of morn
Risest, and with thine arrows of keen light
Dost vanquish darkness, and,—when odorous eve
Spreads 'round her dewy charms,—in vapors clothed
Of hues so gorgeous that they seem to be
Caught from the heavenly portals, sink'st to rest,
To thee I sing.   Who would not sing of thee?
Well wert thou known to primal man as God:
Life is thy gift, by thee the meadows smile,
All song is of thee and the vermeil rose
Thy beams have dyed; and can a god do more?
A God made thee.   Loud sang the heavenly choirs
Chanting His praise, when, from the centre hurled,
The planets circled thee, and from the dense
Primæval mists thou camest forth and shone,
And through the untrodden fields of boundless space,
In chorus singing with thy wheeling worlds
Passed with the speed of thought.   But oh! how long!
What myriad upon myriad ages fled,
Ere yet upon the earth, thy fruitful beams
With heat and light impregnated the seed
Still lifeless hidden in its womd terrene,
And Life, unfathomed, mystic, wonderful,
Appeared to glorify and bless thy ray
Rewarding.   Then, as æons rolled along,
Thy splendours but the course of monsters dread
Did light through deeps tempestuous, till man,—
Formed in the image of thy God, O Sun,—
Was born to empire of the moving world;

And gazing on thee, mindful of thy gifts,
Soon he forgot his Maker and to thee
Bowed worshipping; and straight thou wert a god
With glittering shafts, upon the shadowy race
Waging wide warfare in a varied name :
Hyperion first upon his orb of fire
Flamed 'round the world ; then later fancy saw
Apollo in his golden chariot urge
His steeds, which trampled on the viewless winds,
Across the fields of blue.

               Sun, thou hast gazed
On rising empires, seen the earth stand pale
Before their march resistless, then beheld
Grim Desolation smiling o'er their ruins.
But thou art as of old, in splend'rous guise
Wheeling thy mighty circuit, giving life
To forms innumerable, and in thyself
Art truest symbol of eternity.

How like advancing ocean, Time rolls o'er
Mankind ! who, like some substance cast upon
The restless waters, wearing fast away,
Dissolving in the waves, at length from view
Forever vanishes, nor leaves behind
A single trace to show what once had been.
Not so with thee that art unchanged forever.
Whether thou comest from the orient gates
Clad with the morning, or in western seas
Sinkest to slumber, or when storms are loud
Upon the groaning spheres and murky clouds
Robe thee in night, or when the tempest time
Is past, and thou serenely o'er the sky
Rollest in splendours, thou art still the same,
Eternal, glorious, unfathomed, strong ;
Visible god, throned in immensity.

NATURE PRAISES GOD.

THERE'S not a voice in all the world,—
  However low or loud,—
From the whisper of the daisy
  To the thunder of the cloud,
But speaks the praise of Him Who gave
  The life to all that be,
And, echoing round this radiant sphere
  Sounds on eternally.

The splendour-winged orbs that float
  Upon the waves of light,
The suns that blaze through sapphire deeps,
  Transcendent in their might,
The winds that breathe melodious sighs
  In summer's glowing prime,
The storms that rage when winter binds
  The streams with chains of rime,

Deep calling unto deep, the tones
  Of murmuring waters tell
The glory of the Architect
  Who made all things so well.
Thus Nature speaks; and oh! attune,
  Proud man, thy heart with her,
And yield submission to thy God;
  An humble worshipper.

SING ME A SONG TO-DAY.

Sing me a song to-day
  Softly and low,
Melting my cares away
  With its glad glow.
Sing of the golden prime,
  Childhood's blithe spring,
That fresh, joyous budding time
  Ere blossoming.
When skies were ever blue,
  Days ever clear ;
When hearts were ever true,
  Flowers ever fair.
Careless of all but play,
  Stranger to sorrow ;
Sweet was the world to-day,
  Sweeter each morrow.
Let the high harp awake
  Life in each string,
Soothing my spirit's ache ;
  Sing ! softly sing !
Sing me a song to-day
  Softly and low,
Melting my cares away
  With its glad flow.

TO THE GASPEREAUX.

Happy stream that ever flowest,
    Singing ever,
Many a secret sweet thou knowest,
    Thou wilt never
Tell to man, but tell it only
    To the sea,
Or the stars, that watching lonely,
    Smile on thee.
Dusky lovers roamed beside thee
    In old time,
Blood of dusky warriors dyed thee
    In thy prime.
Scenes, as checkered as the sun ray
    On thy breast,
Sweep thy memory many a one, a
    Fond unrest.
Happy stream that ever flowest,
    Singing ever,
Many a secret tale thou knowest
    Thou wilt never
Tell to man, but tell it only
    To the sea,
Or the stars that watching lonely,
    Smile on thee.

LOVED AND LOST.

———

"'Tis better to have loved and lost
Than never to have loved at all."
—*In Memoriam.*

While wandering o'er life's meadows grand,
　I plucked a rose beside a rill ;
When lo ! a thorn,—by me unscanned,—
Did pierce me sore, and o'er the land
I cast it, but upon my hand
　The perfume lingered still.
The rose I plucked was love ; the thorn
That pierced me was my darling's scorn ;
And memory of that love once dear,
The dulcet perfume lingering there.

———

WHILE YET THY HEART WAS TRUE TO ME.

———

While yet thy heart was true to me,
　And life a field of fairest flowers,
I never thought the time could flee
　That held so many happy hours.

How swiftly sped the moments by,
　Like sunshine glancing o'er the lea,
When not a tear bedimmed the eye
　And thou in life wert all to me !

And can thy breast have grown so cold,
　Thy spirit proved so false to mine,
Thou canst forget those scenes of old
　Which made this mortal life divine ?

To some new lover thou wilt breathe
  Those vows so fondly pledged to me ;
Another's lips from thine receive
  The bliss which mine was wont to be.

Those golden hours from sorrow free,
  When all thy soul was given to me,
Have flown where Fancy's rainbow light
  Plays 'round the brow of Memory.

I WANDER TO-DAY.

I wander to-day with the past
  Along by the many-voiced sea ;
And the roll of the surges upcast,
  Blends strange with each fresh memory.

One eve,—I remember the time,—
  The last smile of day lingered still,
When you promised to ever be mine,
  'Neath the far-spreading oak on the hill.

Thy ringlets were golden in hue,
  A halo of light 'round thy brow ;
Thine eyes, as the summer sky, blue,
  Thy song like the brook in its flow.

But dark frowned the day on thy life,
  And death gave thy soul to the skies ;
And I long, when hath passed ever strife,
  To the place of thy spirit to rise.

PARTING.

Sung at our College Closing, in June, 1894.
AIR: *Juanita.*

Sad, sad to sever
  From the friends we love most dear !
Heart strings must quiver,
  Fall the blinding tear.
But the gloom is lightened
  By the hope we'll meet again ;
Every prospect brightened,
  Riftless friendship's chain.

CHORUS :—

Parting, yes, parting
  From the scenes our love that bind !
Leaving, yet casting
  Lingering looks behind.

Still in full splendour,
  As of old the sun shall shine ;
Moons beam as tender,
  Stars as now divine ;
But the years advancing
  Us shall many changes bring ;
And of *Youth* glad-glancing
  Age shall droop the wing.

But, changeless forever,
  Beams the light of memory ;
True love can never
  From the bosom fly ;
So we'll love and cherish
  These dear days, and scenes, and friends,
Love that shall not perish
  Till life's throbbing ends.

AT MY SISTER'S GRAVE.

Afar in the east shines the rising moon,
　Swift flee the shadows away ;
Softly the winds their low dirges tune,
　Sadly the pine boughs sway.
Here, where the moonshine silvers the mound,
Sister is sleeping her slumber profound,
Deaf to the world and each warring sound,
　Blind to the beams of day.

" Mother, I'm tired, so tired now,
　Tired of life and its pain ;
Kiss me, dear mother, upon my brow,
　Make me your child again.
Now I must sleep, and may never awake,
Mother, dear mother, my cold hands take !"
These latest words from her pale lips brake ;
　Tired, she slumbered then.

Sweetly the sun in the west sank low,
　June smiled amid all her flowers,
And joyous the carollings clear did flow
　Of birds in the leafy bowers ;
When from the bed where the wasted form lay,
Weary and wishing no longer stay,
Trusting in Christ, passed the soul away
　Where golden mansions glow.

Days may arise, shine, and pale to rest,
　Stars shed their splendours afar,
All in their various beauties dressed,
　The seasons may roll their car ;
Never a change in the night of the tomb,
No ray can pierce to that silent gloom,—
Sister, calm sleeping where daisies bloom,
　Nought can thy slumbers mar.

Miscellaneous Poems.

THE DOOM OF THE GODS.

O gods, dethroned and deceased, cast forth, wiped out in a day,
From your wrath is the world released, redeemed from your
    chains men say,
New Gods are crowned in the city, their flowers have broken
    your rods.
They are merciful, clothed with pity, the young compassionate
    gods.
    —*From Swinburne's "Hymn to Proserpine."*

The subject of the following poem is the downfall of the ancient paganism of Greece and Rome,
on the introduction of Christianity. The object is
primarily the glorification of the latter religion, and
secondarily of the mighty bards of old,—especially
of Homer,—whose compositions have in reality made
the Olympian deities,—in name at least,—immortal,
and created the sublime and beautiful mythic realm
wherein they have dwelt and ruled with antique sway
since they have ceased to live and reign in the real
world of men.

I sing of gods whose immortality
Was won by men who at their shrines adored.

O love of beauty, heavenly power, vouchsafe
To tune my voice in somewhat loftier tone,
To celebrate the most supremest type
Of beauty, moulded by the minds that wove
O'er Grecian mountains and o'er Latian plains
A spell that clothed them with divinity.

The loveliness that comes when day smiles out
Refulgent on the world, or when the night
Glooms in her solemn majesty, and all
The soul delights in of the seasons' range :
The life-awaking Spring, the gorgeous bloom
Of Summer and the Autumn's perfect prime
Tell to the mind that ever round us yet
Hover the spirits of the bards of old.
As when at night within the darkling deep,
The sky with all her glittering host of stars
Is mirrored, and the mariner beholds
The all-ensphering heaven, he knows and feels
The universal presence of a God.

Upon that day when Mary's Son redeemed
Man from the power of Hell, on many-peaked
Olympus, in the golden house of Jove,
The gods with all their consanguinity
Were gathered ; for the earth, and air and sea,
And realms beneath the earth, by force did yield
Their various rulers up.   High on a throne
Resplendent all with gold, whose dazzling form
Blazed like a mirror in the noon-day sun,
Hiding its structure, but in bold relief
Showing the mighty occupant, He sat,
The All-Ruling Sire ; the head, whose awful nod
Shook earth to her foundations, on his breast
Declined, a leaden weight ; the crown had fallen
Upon the jasper pavement and there lay,
A beam of light upon a sanguine sea.
His hand no longer held the glowing bolt,
Which, falling, idly lay anear his feet,
Lifeless and cold.   Beside him Juno sat
In deepest sorrow, with her clasped hands
Reclining on her lap ; her head upraised
And looks cast forward and steadfast, as though

Through golden pillar and amethystine wall
The vision pierced, encountering far beyond
The horrid features of Despair rise up
From utmost chaos.   Her ambrosial locks
Fell o'er her snowy shoulders and her breast,
And swayed but with its heaving.   Many more
Were there of the divine ones ; girded still
In adamantine mail, the warrior Mars,
But shorn of all his fury ; trident-armed
Neptune, and the wise Aegis-Bearing One,
Minerva, but her Aegis was bereft
Of its Gorgonian terrors ; sad she stood
With hand upon her upright massy spear,
While from beneath the helm, her tresses gold
Streamed backward, and majestic sorrow dimmed
Her large blue eye.   The Queen of Love was there ;
And He, the Archer of the Silver Bow,
Apollo, lovely in immortal youth,
Around whose form the Sacred Sisters Nine
Gathered with all their tuneful harps unstrung.
While, thronging the long corridors, or clinging
Around the lofty columns, or the throne
Of some celestial power, all the beings
That ever flamen taught or poet dreamed,—
Dryad and Faun, and Satyr, Grace and Nymph,
And many a Naiad fair,—their native haunts
Deserting, there were gathered.   Oft before
Had Jove's high dwelling brightened with the glow
Of deities assembled, when the world
Youthful, obeyed them all in youth and knew
Naught but obedience ; then celestial might
Was in their limbs, and glory all divine
Gleamed from their faces ; now how changed ! how
          changed !
Sorrow possessed each heart, and on each brow
Despair was written, while a silence deep

Brooded like magic spell upon them all.
But grief cannot remain in silence long,
But must expression find, when the first stroke
That numbs the soul hath passed ; for words bring balm
To pangs they body forth ; so when we hear
The sad relation of another's woe,
He seems to share and lighten thus our own ;
And weakest spirits first this comfort seek.
" Apollo, sing some sorrow-laden song,
That these black hours, which stagnate into years,
May move more quickly by."   So sighing, spake
Calliope, and turned appealing looks
Upon her deity ; but no response
Parted his lips ; and in short interval
Again she cried : " Apollo, sing ! oh sing !"
At this he lifted up his head and gazed
Around, beholding every vision bent
Upon him ; even the far-piercing eye
Of the still awful Jove in mute appeal
Respake the words : " Apollo, sing ! oh sing !"
Apollo answered not ; but o'er the harp
His melody-awaking fingers passed.
Thrice he essayed the unwilling strain to raise,
Thrice failed his voice and touch ; then straight he flung
The shell aside, and breathed his accents thus :
" I cannot sing, for tongue and string alike
Refuse their duty ; but I may the tale
Relate of my dread downfall and mayhap
This aching time will haste its slow career.
Throned on the blazing car which bore of old
Hyperion, through the sapphire orient gates
I late came forth bringing the blushing morn.
Far through the limitless demesnes of space,
Rushing with thunder speed, my chariot passed ;
The ethereal coursers from their nostrils blowing
The flaming hours, and with their dreadless hoofs

Treading the ambient winds, and bearing day
To mortals and immortals, chasing night,
That fled before in terror, to his cave
Deep in the Occidental ; on, on, on
They sped, until with tireless feet they trod
The empyrean, when behind I heard
A sound as of the sweeping of great wings,
Or as a forest on some mountain side
Swayed by the tempest, when Euroclydon
Wakes raging.   Rearward straight my vision turned,
And lo ! an unknown one, whom like a god
I'd call, but for a god he seemed too bright,
Too glorious ; rainbows circled all his form,
And, widely waving from his shoulders, wings
Supported him ; before him, the right hand
Did grasp a blade, that like the lightning's beam,
Jagged streamed forth afar.   His countenance
Majestic past all utterance ; Jove might ne'er
Gaze fearless on that brow.   Onward he came,
Doubling my coursers' speed, his mighty vans,
Like two great clouds of purest white, outspread
Fanning the air to whirlwinds.   He o'ertook
Me soon, and with a voice as of the sea
Lab'ring in tempest, " Phœbus from thy place
Descend and yield thy flaming car to me,
The minister of Him who reigns supreme.
The old gods are too weak for sovereignty,
And from beneath their feeble rule hath passed
The empire of the universe ; descend !"
And by his word, stricken as Phaeton
By Jove's hurled thunder, down through the abyss,
Earthward I fell—down ! down ! the ærial mists
Smote on my form, as, by my horrid speed,
They seemed to harden ; till, with dizzy brain,
Upon Olympus' top I ceased my flight,
Leaving my coursers guided by new hands

And terrible. But whence that being came,
Where nurtured, by what hidden power sent forth,
I know it not." Then with a sigh that choked
His further utterance, Phœbus ceased ; and straight
The Harmonious Sisters seized their lyres and strung,
And singing soothed awhile each paining heart.
" Mourn for the beauty gone, the glory lost."
This the refrain ; and when it died away,
The voice of Maia's Winged Son was heard
Cleaving the silence and his accents these :
" The power that hath unsceptered us, to me
Hath been revealed. Thou knowest, O father Jove,
Thrice hath the Lord of day through Scorpius passed,
Since One within the far Judean land,—
His birth was marked by all the elements,—
Although a mortal, did proclaim himself
God and the Son of God. But not in guise
Godlike he came, on sunbright car enthroned,
Begirt with flaming hosts ; nay, nor in state
Of earthly monarch, clad in starry splendor
Of jewelled robes keen sparkling, but was born
In lowly manger 'mid sweet breathing kine
That knelt adoring ; meekness and gentleness
'Bode with Him ever ; more than human love
He bore for those by sin and woe oppressed ;
And many hearts were by His precepts turned
To offer prayer at other shrines than ours.
This day, the clouds dividing with swift wing,
O'er land and sea toward Tithonus' realm,
I sped ; but paused above the wind-swept plain
That erst knew Ilium. Fond remembrance came
Of deeds by gods and god-like heroes done,
When gods were young and great, and ruled unchecked,
And humankind were like to them in might.
Thence onward passed, and on the formless winds
Riding, I came, where, on her ancient hills

Jerusalem gleamed forth in regal pride.
When sounds, such as near reached mine ear before,
Came on the breeze ; and from the horizon far,
Uprose in rank on rank of order true,
In countless myriads, a shining host
Of beings never viewed by heavenly ken.
Winnowing with plumes immense the yielding air,
They came, thought-speeded, with great faces turned,—
Oh, how impotent are the loftiest words
E'er syllabled by created tongue, to tell
What beauty and what majesty sublime
Shone radiant on them !—towards Jerusalem ;
Each orb of sight fixed steadfast on a hill,
The goal of their advance ; and so intent
Their eager gaze, unnoticed me they passed.
As birds, that, numberless, with steady wing
Circle some broad based tower e'er they alight,
To rear new homes when Spring bids earth awake,
So in vast gyres moving, these at last
Encircled all the hill, rank above rank,
Receding as they rose, till high above
Calvaria's mount they formed a living crown.
No sound arose as that ethereal host,
With folded pinion and transfixed gaze,
Hung in mid-air.   My sight did follow theirs ;
And round the hill and from the city gates
Still pouring, multitudinous as the leaves
In Latmian forests, a tumultuous mass
Of mortals came to look upon the pangs
Of the pale Galilean, on a cross
Fixed writhing in enormous agonies.
Curses and mockeries, and insults vile
Were yielded by the crowd ; when suddenly
The sun was gloomed in unforetold eclipse,
And darkness rushed across the trembling orb,
Making a dreadful silence ; broken soon

As the deep cry rang from the suffering lips :
" Eli, eli lama sabathani."
Another pause succeeded ; then again,
" 'Tis finished," was the cry, for death was come.
Then earth in horrible convulsion shook
Groaning in earthquake travail ; and huge rocks,
Torn from their beds, hurled echoing around,
Made universal din ; and from the tombs,
The dead, long mouldering, in their cerements
Came forth, a ghastly band, to tread once more
Paths erst familiar.   From its body freed,
The Prophet's spirit lingered not but rose
Upward as borne by its unbounded will,
To that aerial band which moveless hung
Like cloud that waits the breeze by summer blown.
Forthwith in adoration every brow
Declined ; and from the serried ranks arose
A song of triumph loud but strangely sweet ;
As nor Apollo, nor the Muses Nine
Forth from their throbbing throats have ever poured.
Then when the melody had died away,
He Who but one short hour's space before
Had been the weakest and the scorn of men,
But now the adored of the supernal powers,
With majesty spake : " All is finished now,
The grave is conquered, death of sting bereft,
Hell's empire overthrown, and man made heir
To an eternal glory.   The false gods
Who have seduced his spirit from the right,
To them unworthy worship, must be driven
From all their realms ; that earth no more deny
Me and My Father.   Ministers of light,
Forth on your mission ! may none tarriance show."
They heard His voice ; and on the nimble wing
Wheeling, like sun rays from the centre cast
They tracked the course of all the winds of heaven.

The event we sadly know ; and who can tell
That our dread conquerors may hither come
To this, our latest refuge ?"   At that word
All eyes instinct toward the portal rolled.
When lo ! a light as of the rising sun
Shone in the palace ; and the galleries,
And columned vistas, and colossal walls
Glowed as the clouds that cradle the young Dawn.
And, as the day flames upward to his noon,
The lustre grew, till every countenance
Its wonder witnessed and its deep dismay ;
When, through the lofty archway's ample space,
The Living Splendor entered.   From its form
Such radiance came as e'en immortal sight
Could scarce endure.   His stature passing far
Earth's hugest sons, or in the northland dark,
Whose wondrous deeds in many a saga live,
The brood of Jotunheim.   Typhœus dire
He might have seized and with one hand unnerved.
Around his head a golden crown blazed forth
And seemed a circling fire.   The majesty
Of stainless strength, with passions all unmixed,—
Save of a love lit on no earthly shrine,—
Reigned on his countenance ; and plume on plume,
Down from his shining shoulders, his vast vans
Like alabaster towers, on either side
Guarded his form ; nor sword, nor sheltering shield
Bore he, nor of such argument had need
To aid his conquering glance ; and every god,
All mute before this flaming messenger,
Instinctive waited for his words of fate.
Nor long ; for like some organ swelling vast
Its volumed tones and deep, the Glory spake :
" The doom pronounced by Heaven's Eternal King
On you, now justly driven from those thrones,
Whereon for ages ye have fed mankind

With dire deceits and warped the living truth,
Hear and abide !   Ye are adulterous gods ;
And all unworthy 'twere that man should bow
And worship more at such polluted shrines,
Offending the Most High.   No longer then
Your reigns endure ; and coming years shall bring
No hope of rule returned ; but, since the minds
Many, that to the Olympian altars bent
Adoring, drew an inspiration grand,
And with their concourse of immortal thoughts,
An intellectual realm of glory formed,
Sublime and beautiful ; where lovely forms,
And forms majestic, heroes and heroines,
And mighty demi-gods, forever move
Amid those flowers which, born of Time,
Shall bloom the comrades of Eternity.
Thither ye shall retire ; and, while mind
Endures through untold ages yet to come,
Over that wondrous land when man shall tread
He pales before the blazing bolt of Jove
And feels the trembling spheres confess his nod.
Still in that mythic world as here of old,
Apollo's steeds shall usher in the day,
And fire the western clouds at eventide ;
Great cities quake before the Warrior's voice,
And fall beneath his spear ; and Pallas breathe
Her words of wisdom, and Diana roam,
Brightening the groves with rays of Chastity.
But, nevermore may odorous incense rise
From the altars reared to you ; and men shall blend
Their voices, swelling loud the tuneful praise
Of the true God, eternal, infinite,
Perfect in wisdom, goodness, and in mercy.
The past is dead ; a newer, better time
Dawns on a world, freed from the iron rule
Of gods whose noblest attribute was strength.

A better time, when love, displacing might,
Dwells chiefly ; and as ages roll along
Shall strengthen, till, all nations and all tribes
Soothed by its power, with evil passions lulled
To endless rest, a single glorious hymn
From all the earth shall rend the echoing skies,
Attuned to God ; and universal peace,—
Unknown since Eden's lords obedient moved,—
Shall with a flowery wreath the planet bind.
Depart, O heirs of sorrow, to that world,
By blind old Homer made so long ago,
Where change may enter not." He spake, and straight
He stood alone upon the verdurous height,
His snowy pinions folded to his side,
His shining hands clasped steadfast, while his head,
Decked with its crown of light, was slowly bent
As if in sorrow.   Musing, last he spake :
" Why should a shade regretful touch my frame
For these fall'n powers ? All which they inspired
Of beauty lives forever, and their reign
Of myriad ages never yet removed
A single pang entailed on human hearts."
He ceased ; and spreading his wide-shadowing plumes,
And floating down the day-star's western track,
Vanished and left to night the world redeemed.

In that same hour, across the orb there rang
From Grecian valleys to the Lybian sands,
Beyond the Pillars to the Blessed Isles,
Thence o'er the listening ocean wastward far,
Where Cotapaxi's mountain roaring shakes
A continent and with ambitious flame
Daunts the pale stars, and every nation heard
The far resounding voice : " Great Pan is dead."
And where Olympus' form slopes to the sea,

Upon the forest lyre the sad winds smote,
Waking melodious murmurs that swelled sweet
And soft and mournful till the notes conjoined
In one weird cry · " Great Pan is dead, is dead,"*
Then sank again to silence as before.

LIFE'S CHARM FLOWN.

There's not a joy this world can give like that it takes away,
When the glow of early thought declines in feelings dull decay.
—*Byron*

O what is life worth when its charm is departed,
    When the soul's sensibility's deadened and o'er ;
When things once so pleasing pass by unregarded,
    And the heart throbs responsive to beauty no more ?

I am not as I was : in the seasons that slumber
    With the sepulchred Past, Nature's every refrain
Gave to memory exquisite joys without number,
    " Like wax to receive and like marble retain."

In rapture I'd gaze on the splendours all golden
    Of sunset wide flaming the skies in the west ;
And by spell of the beauty in ecstasy holden,
    I watched till the world in night's mantle was dressed.

The cold, silent moon in her majesty sweeping
    O'er her star-studded pathway, pale empress of night,
The planets their vigils unceasingly keeping,
    Of old ever yielded me purest delight.

* See the legend in Plutarch.

The wind breathing gently o'er mountain and meadow,
  Giving soft voices to whispering boughs,
The placid lake checkered with sunshine and shadow,
  And songs that in deep glades the echoes arouse.

I loved Nature's calms ; but my strongest affection
  Awoke when in terror she shrouded her form :
When a cloud-compelled gloom hid the day-star's com-
    plexion,
  And a heart-thrilling silence preluded the storm.

My being was stirred with sublime exultation,
  As the lightnings blazed out dealing death to the
    gloom,
And the thunder's voice spake to the trembling crea-
    tion
  In anger as roaring the last note of doom ;

And the tempest rushed forth and the forest was
    shaken,
  While pines, thunder-smitten were hurled to the
    ground,
And clamorous crows by the blast overtaken
  Were whirled with the withered leaves helpless
    around.

Yea ! Nature had voices, articulate voices
  That spake to me then as friend speaketh to friend ;
Their accents are dumb ; and my spirit rejoices
  No more in that converse so sweet to attend.

Of old, my young mind with its fancies o'erteeming,
  Would people each grot, every glade, every glen
With numberless forms of rare beauty, each seeming
  As real to me as my friends among men.

Oh what is life worth when its charm is departed,
   The soul's sensibility deadened and o'er ?
When things which once thrilled us are passed unre-
     garded,
   And the heart swells responsive to beauty no more ?